REFERENCES AND CREDIT

The geographical and topographical description of the areas covered in this story are taken from **Lands of the Bible** by J.W. McGarvey, copyright 1880, publisher The Standard Publishing Company of Cincinnati, Ohio. Mr. McGarvey traveled the areas.

The photos for the front and back covers were purchased from istockphoto.com.

Special thanks to Mr. Fred McKinney for giving verbal consent to include his poem, **Just Like That Shunammite.** The poem is included at the end of this story and more notes about the scriptural references are given just before the poem.

Much thanks to Mr. Eric Hammersley for constructing the front and back cover of this story.

THE SHUNAMMITE WOMAN
MEANINGS OF NAMES, SCRIPTURE RERERENCES
AND POSSIBLE DATES FOR PLACES, EVENTS AND
PEOPLE'S LIVES

Women's names: Bina which means intelligence,
understanding, wisdom.

Ashira means wealthy.

Nava means beautiful.

Men's names: Oren means pine tree.

Nathan means giver.

Shunammite's servant perhaps an Ethiopian: Palus means
humble.

Rada means our helper.

Shunem: 1 Sam. 28:4 1056 BC.

Solomon: 1 Kings 1:1-3 1015 BC.

Solomon lived and wrote Proverbs 31 in 1015 BC. He
wrote Ecclesiastes in 977 BC.

Solomon perhaps died in 975 BC as the Holmon Bible
shows Rehoboam taking the throne in that

year.

Joshua mentions Shunem in the tribe of Issachar in Joshua 19:18 1444 BC.

The Shunammite's story is found in 2 Kings 4:8-37, 895 BC according to Holmon Bible.

Elisha warned her of approaching famine in 2 Kings 8:1-2 892 BC and she journeys to the land

of the Philistines and returns seven years later in 885 BC in the reference 2 Kings 8:3-6.

Joram over Israel in 896-884 BC. Called Jehoram in 2 Kings 3:1; 9:23-24. Jehoram was also

the son of Jehoshaphat in 2 Kings 8:16, a different person than Joram.

Jehoshaphat over Judah 954-891 BC.

Jehoram over Judah 891-883 BC.

Internet says Omri over Israel 893-883 BC or 885-874 BC.

Halley's Bible Handbook

Elisha started 850 BC under reign of Jehoram in 2 Kings 3:1, 11 and continued through reign of

Jehu and Jehoahaz, dying in reign of Joash in 2 Kings 13:14-20 around 800 BC.

Elisha was gentle, gracious, diplomatic and his miracles are recorded in 2 Kings 2,4,5,6, and 7.

Holmon Bible says he died in 856 BC.

Elisha lived in Abelmeholah in 906 BC in 1 Kings 19:16.

In 2 Kings 3:1 Jehoram began to reign 12 years, 896-884 BC.

Israelite king Jehoram in 850 BC.

Elisha 852-814 BC, or 850-800 BC. See above for 906 BC in Abelmeholah.

Abishag in 1 Kings 1:3 probably 1015 BC. She was perhaps a teenager.

In 2 Kings 4 perhaps 895 BC Abishag would be 135 years old.

FORWARD

The Shunammite Woman lived in Old Testament

times in the Bible. The dates of 2 Kings 4 and 2 Kings 8

where her story is found is most likely 896 to 884 BC.

With the exception of this biblical account, her life

happenings as written here are fictional but do serve as

being consistent with her outstanding character. Money in

the form of coins was not in use at that time so in keeping

with the history of that period, the gold in the form of

bands or rings is maintained for money.

Perhaps contractions in speech were used in Bible

times and that will be the case in this story as it seems

awkward to not use them in conversations herein. Miles

for distances and feet instead of cubits will be used

throughout.

As the scriptures reveal, King Joram reigned twelve

years over Israel (see page one for scripture reference).

Due to the fictional elements in the story the author must

extend that time to fifteen years due to the gift of two horses to The Shunammite Woman by the king and the three years of time elapsed before The Shunammite Woman has the child promised to her by Elisha, the prophet. The child is five years old when he dies of the sunstroke. After that there is the seven years of famine. As you can see this adds up to fifteen years.

18,998 Words

THE SHUNAMMITE WOMAN

BY

LARRY HAMMERSLEY

"My Lady, Bina, I fear for your safety going to Sidon alone. If only you had a husband," Palus, the Shunammite woman's servant said.

Bina's heart was touched, always by her Ethiopian servant's concern for her.

"The Lord will be with me. The road is well traveled. Everyone will be going to their vast market. Ships will be coming from Egypt and other places laden with goods before they proceed on to Ephesus. I must have the wonderful seeds from Egypt. The barley, wheat, corn and rye are said to grow in any soil."

"Nonetheless, if I may say so, why can't I go with you?" Palus asked.

"I am concerned for Abishag. She's over a hundred years old and I want you to check on her every other day. She trusts you as much as she does me," Bina answered.

"You are always such a caring person," Palus said.

"Thank you, Palus. I don't know what I'd do without you," she said, gently resting her hand on his chocolate bicep.

"You're too kind. I'll prepare your wagon for your early morning departure." She watched Palus take his long strides to the barn.

Bina walked the short distance down the street in the center of Shunem to Abishag's home. She adjusted her garment to clear the dusty road better. Abishag was sitting on her porch, beaming a smile on her wrinkled face as Bina approached.

"Oh, Bina, come here for a hug," she said, extending her boney arms.

"Always for you," Bina said and bent over to accept the hug.

"And everyone else. Your reputation reaches far and wide."

"I will be leaving in the morning for Sidon. Palus will be checking on you every other day," she whispered in Abishag's ear. Her faculties were still sharp at 135.

"Such a dangerous trip."

"The market will last a month. I intend to be there when the ship arrives from Egypt. Besides the seeds I need, they will have the new bronze cookware. I've heard that nothing sticks to it during cooking," Bina said.

"Hurry back."

"I will be back in time for the semiannual feast I prepare for all of Shunem. It will take two days to get there, one day at Sidon and two days to return. Palus will be interested in all your stories about King David and King Solomon," Bina said, squeezing Abishag's skinny shoulders.

"I have plenty of stories. You've heard them so many times. I'm sorry I repeat myself so much."

"I never grow tired of hearing them. I must go. Palus will be by tomorrow." Bina gave Abishag one last hug and left.

*   *   *

That evening Palus had the wagon ready. He greased the axels, gave extra feed to her wagon horse and constructed the secret compartment on the underside of the wagon's bed. She would store her gold and certified weights there. Strong ropes for securing the wares she would bring back, a protective covering for those wares, feed for the horse, food for herself, and water for herself and the horse, rounded out the supplies she needed to make the trip to Sidon. Palus even included spare wagon parts in case of a breakdown.

She owned two horses, one she would use for the trip and one that Palus would use to till the south fields of Esdraelon while she was gone. Fondness resided in her heart for the Israelite king, Joram, who insisted on giving her the horses despite her offering him gold. His story was that the two horses weren't strong enough to serve as war horses. Bina was a fair judge of horse flesh and these horses were the strongest she'd seen. They were well-behaved, perfect for riding, pulling ploughs, wagons and giving an audible warning if strangers approached. She was also a good judge of character and knew Joram wanted to show he wasn't like his father, Ahab or his mother, Jezebel.

The next morning, when the sun hadn't cleared the mountains beyond the Jordan River yet, Bina said her departing remarks to Palus.

"I should make it to Tyre before dark. It will be good to see Nava again. I'll stay with her tonight and then make Sidon in time to seek for an inn to relax until the next morning."

"My Lady, Bina, I wish you a safe trip. Hurry back," Palus said. He checked the wagon one last time.

"I'll be back the evening of the fifth day."

As Bina travelled through the gap between Jezreel and her home in Shunem, she thought of the recent history. The Philistines had encamped in her village and went on to Mt. Gilboa and killed King Saul. Elijah had called fire from heaven on another occasion, or so she had heard, barely a year ago. He had passed his powers on to Elisha. She had never seen either Elijah or Elisha. She accepted, through faith, the story of Elijah being taken to heaven in a fiery chariot. Silently, she thanked the Lord for her living in an exciting time when God's power was displayed often.

Bina could see Mt. Carmel, although nearly twenty miles distant, enshrouded in early morning fog. Along her route she stopped at a clear spring to allow her horse a drink before proceeding to the base of Mt. Carmel where she would turn northward towards Tyre.

Late afternoon she enjoyed the cool breeze coming off the Great Sea just west of the road heading toward Tyre.

Ahead she saw a wagon stopped and tilted at an odd angle. A man squatted beside a wheel which lay flat in the road. The axel rested in the dirt. A woman, presumably his wife, rested at the side of the road. Bina saw she was great with child. Distress creased lines in her face as well as her husband's. Their horse periodically glanced back, his ears perking and then lying back against his head. Bina pulled to a stop and stepped down.

"Sir, may I help you?"

The man smiled, but his countenance remained downcast.

"I doubt it. I've lost the pin on the axel and don't have a spare. The wagon is heavy and you're a. . . "He stopped and seemed embarrassed.

". . . a woman," Bina finished.

"I am sorry. I did not mean to offend." He looked down.

"I am not offended, I assure you. The road is well travelled. Hasn't anyone offered to help you?"

"I'm afraid not."

"I have spare axel pins, the size you need. Unload your wagon and it will be light enough for us to lift."

"It will still be heavy and my wife is in no condition to help." He said.

"Please, we must try. I have an idea, a simple one."

The man agreed, but Bina could still see doubt on his face as he took a deep breath without making eye contact with her.

They placed the wagon items to the side of the road. Bina fetched a pin from the storage box and returned to the broken wagon.

"Stand the wheel up against the side of the wagon and we will lift it while your wife can roll it to line up the wheel with the axel and you can put it in place and one of us can insert the pin into the axel," Bina said.

"But the wagon is still heavy and my wife shouldn't exert herself," the man said.

"My husband, I can do it. I won't have to lift at all. This wonderful woman looks strong to me," his wife said, rising to her feet with some difficulty.

"It seems I'm out voted," he smiled, this time without skepticism in his voice.

The man propped the wheel to a vertical position against the wagon and near the axel. Bina gave the axel pin to him and signaled that she stood ready to lift. They positioned themselves on opposite sides of the axel and his wife grasped the rim of the wheel. Simultaneously, Bina and the man lifted the wagon. Bina equaled the efforts of the man as the axel aligned with the hub of the wheel. His wife rolled the wheel in place and the man, with one arm, positioned the wheel onto the axel. Worry drained from his face as he witnessed Bina's efforts exceeded his during the insertion of the wheel onto the axel. Gently, Bina allowed the axel and wheel take the wagon's weight and the man inserted the pin into the axel.

"I think you're stronger than me," he said, his breathing slightly labored.

"Oh, I wouldn't say that," Bina said, stepping back and beginning to help load their supplies back onto the wagon.

After helping with loading their wagon, Bina prepared to mount her own wagon.

"My manners. My wife's name is Kezia and I am Shapan. We are of the tribe of Zebulon headed for Tyre to a midwife there."

"I'm Bina of the tribe of Issachar."

"The Shunammite Woman? We've heard so much about you. As the queen of Sheba said of Solomon, 'the half has not been told of you,'" Shapan said.

"Please, I am not worthy of such praise," Bina said, her cheeks feeling flushed.

"Oh, but you are. You're headed our way. Let's travel together."

"Certainly. I will be proceeding on to Sidon for the market which starts day after tomorrow. I'll be staying with a friend in Tyre."

Bina enjoyed talking to Shapan and Kezia. It made the trip seem shorter. As they approached Tyre, the road was cut out of a solid cliff face. The road was wide and safe if traveled in daylight. The drop from the road to the blue sea to their left was 200 feet. The sea far below was in constant motion. After coming down from the cliff face they encountered a channel of water that turned a water wheel. The stream of water, nearly as wide as a river, supplied the island city of Tyre with cool, clear water. Only three miles to go and they would be in Tyre. Daylight was fading fast but they arrived before darkness fell. Bina bid her new friends goodbye and headed for Nava's modest hut near water's edge.

Bina spotted her perched on a stone block near the road in front of her house. Nava, meaning beautiful, was the perfect name for her. Her hair, in golden ringlets, cascaded down the front of her maroon wrap. The blond hair framed a face that had a youthful blushing innocence about it. Bina was not at all jealous that Nava's beauty far exceeded her own, quite the opposite, she glowed inside that the Lord had blessed her friend so. Her wonderful character matched her beauty. Nava spotted her, sprang from her perch and ran to meet her, arms outstretched.

"Oh, Bina, I was so worried you wouldn't make it before dark. I knew you'd come to Sidon's market." She nearly bowled Bina over.

"Nava, your beauty seems greater as always," Bina said.

"Not like yours. This beautiful coal black hair is much lovelier than mine," Nava said, caressing Bina's hair as they broke their embrace.

"You always have the right words. Bless you."

"Here, follow me and we'll pull your horse and wagon into the barn. Plenty of feed and water for your fine looking horse."

"King Joram gave me two horses he claimed were reject war horses. He refused to take payment. I can't imagine he has better horses for the host of Israel than the ones he gave me."

"It is twenty-four miles to Sidon so you can make it easily and find a place to stay before nightfall. I'm looking forward to your semi-annual feast in Shunem," Nava said, unhitching Bina's horse and leading him to a roomy stall with plenty of straw, feed and water.

Bina followed Nava to her dwelling and enjoyed a meal and visit. She had not married yet but talked of her love interest, a soldier in Joram's host. She feared for his safety.

"Bina, it's time you found a husband. What are you? Two and twenty?"

"Yes. I'm very busy with the farm. Besides, a woman just doesn't go out and ask a man if he's interested in starting a family," Bina said.

"I have a feeling the right man will come along soon."

"Nava, are you trying to act like Elisha or one of the other prophets?"

"No," Nava laughed.

The time went too fast as they turned in for the night.

Mid morning the next day Bina said goodbye to Nava, promising she would stop again on her way back. Nava expressed her concern for Bina's safety, her traveling alone and having valuable goods in her wagon for the trip back to Shunem. Bina repeated her faith that the Lord would see to her safe return.

Excitement rose in Bina as she journeyed on. The weather was perfect, a cool wind blowing in from The Great Sea dispelling some of the harsh rays of the sun.

At the half way point between Tyre and Sidon, she passed through Zarapheth where about twenty years ago a great drought grasped the land. Elijah performed a miracle for the widow and her son by replenishing her barrel of meal constantly for a year until the rains came ending the drought. Fascinated by God's work she wished for the identity of the widow, but alas, Elijah had been taken to heaven by the fiery chariot and the woman's identity remained unknown for the present. If she had the time, she could enquire while here to learn of the woman's name and hear her story.

As she approached Sidon she stopped to eat an apple Nava had given her. She gave her horse a few small ears of corn. Nearby was the harbor of Sidon and she could see ships in the harbor from Egypt. They bobbed gently in the near calm waters. She could make out men loading wagons with a variety of goods for transport into the inner city for tomorrow's market.

Nava had recommended an inn near the harbor and she headed that way. The sun seemed a red ball floating on the Great Sea in the west, turning the peaks of Mount Hermon to gold in the east and she anticipated a night of rest before a busy morning at the market the next day. The inn was already nearly full as she paid the keeper and pulled her horse and wagon into a spacious barn that joined hard to the inn. She would rent a two-wheeled cart the next morning, one she could pull with some effort to and from the nearby market. The inn had employed a couple of Roman soldiers to protect their goods as they brought them from the market for storage in their wagons. The market would be busy and crowded, much too crowded for traversing with traveling wagons and horses.

The next morning, after she had breakfast at the inn, she picked up a map provided by the inn. It showed the market layout. As she feared, the location of the booth with the barley, wheat, corn and rye seeds were at the far end of the market. It would take all her strength to pull the cart with heavy bags of seeds through the narrow alleys and streets to get back to the inn. Bina knew she would only have time for two trips, one for cookware and one for the many bags of seeds, before nightfall. She would stick to her schedule of staying one day before departing for home.

She pulled the empty cart to the cookware seller as it was at the edge of the market nearest the inn. As she approached she knew the cookware seller was dishonest. She recognized he was using false weights, not certified weights like the ones she brought along. Apparently, he had very few customers, as others may have spotted the false weights too. She called to mind a proverb of Solomon saying "a false balance is abomination to the Lord: but a just weight is his delight." She approached and the man looked up, his face brightening at the prospect of a rare customer.

"Sir, I see your business is very poor. I can tell you why," Bina said.

"Oh, and who made you a judge of my business?" The man's voice was laced with anger as Bina picked up one of his weights.

"Put that down. Those are certified weights, very valuable," he said, reaching for the weight Bina had picked up. She jerked away from his grasping hand.

"Then you won't mind me comparing your weights with these truly certified ones from Jerusalem," Bina said, reaching in her pocket and pulling out two golden bands with the Jerusalem shop's official stamp.

The man's eyes grew big as he stared at Bina's weights.

"If your weights are correct then your balance will rest even. If they are not then I expect your weights will be lighter than mine, much to your favor."

"Please no," the man pleaded, resting his hand on Bina's, before she tested his weights with her true ones. A man with a red turban stepped forward. Bina knew him as one of the men who circulated through the market place to keep the sellers honest.

"Please do. If your weights are true then you have nothing to worry about, Gadi," the official said. Bina handed the official her two weights. He looked at them and smiled through his closely cropped salt and pepper beard.

"This lady has true weights. I recognize the Jerusalem shop's emblem." He tested the certified weights with Gadi's weights. Sure enough, Gadi's weights were lighter. Anger flashed through the official's face and he grabbed Gadi's lose fitting wrap.

"I am throwing you out Gadi, and confiscating your goods."

"Please, sir. Gadi has the finest of cookware from Egypt's Delta region. I will loan him two of my weights for today. I'm sure he will make restitution to his former customers. Is that right, Gadi?" Bina asked.

"Oh, yes, for sure," Gadi quickly replied, taking a deep breath.

"You should thank this lady. She saved you from a prison in Jerusalem where you would wait for, no doubt, a sentence of death. I suggest you sell her some of your best bronze cookware at bargain prices, and don't waste any time seeking out the people you've cheated."

"Bargains from Gadi won't be necessary. I'm sure he will set things right," Bina said, casting a questioning look Gadi's way.

"Oh, yes, I will. The customers are not far away. I'll ask this kind lady to watch my goods while I go find them. Would you be so kind. . ?"

"Bina. Yes, and I will select what I came for while you are gone."

The man with the red turban seemed satisfied and left to check other booths and merchants.

Gadi hurried away and Bina looked over his merchandise. She found it high quality. There was cookware of all sizes made from iron, copper, and bronze. She had plenty of iron utensils which were expensive in themselves so she concentrated on the bronze ware. She gazed at a large kettle made of bronze and feared a great price would be asked, but she needed something that size because her festival kept growing.

She used her spare weights on the bronze ware and loaded the cookware in her cart and by the time her selections were made, Gadi returned.

"The customers were happy that I settled up with them and intend to send other customers my way, especially when I mentioned certified weights. When I said your name a few of them knew you were the Shunammite Woman from Shunem."

"Do you see that honesty is the best policy?" Bina asked.

"Yes, for sure and I probably owe you my life. Have you gotten everything you wanted?" Gadi asked, looking at her cart.

"Almost, and I hope you trust I used my weights in selecting the bronze ware."

"I certainly trust you. You said almost. What else do you need?" Gadi asked.

"One item which I doubt I could afford and have money left for seed."

"What would that be?"

Bina pointed at the large kettle.

"Why don't you pay me for the other cookware and go get your seed. See how much money you have left and we'll talk then. Actually, I don't think I can sell the kettle. Customers don't want anything that big and I'm tired of carrying it around."

Bina agreed and when she handed Gadi her payment in gold bands, he drew a deep breath.

"Your payment is gladly accepted. I hope you are not traveling alone with your gold."

"Well, the Lord will protect me, besides I may not have much left after today. I wish I had brought more after seeing that large pot."

"You must be very wealthy, and thieves will kill you for a much smaller portion of gold than what you probably have," Gadi remarked.

"I've been blessed. Our ancestors mined gold from Sheba in Arabia and it was kept down to my parents' time. They are both deceased."

"I am sorry. Looks like a mob of customers coming this way. Please come back at the end of the day," Gadi said, turning and dealing with his customers.

Bina bowed her head and smiled. She pulled her cart back to the inn and loaded her cookware onto her wagon and fed her horse. She hurried back with her empty cart and headed for the seed market area. It was mid day and the sun beamed mercilessly on her face. When she arrived she was dismayed at the vastness of the seed marketers. She did not hurry but examined the seed of the crops she wanted to plant. The merchants had a bag of each kind that was open so that customers could visually inspect what they hoped to purchase. She spent nearly two hours selecting the barley, wheat, rye and corn. The bags of all of them together were heavy. On a whim she bought a small bag of date seeds too. After she paid for everything she went to pull her cart and found it so heavy that she could barely move it. At that rate it would be dark by the time she managed to get it back to the inn. Gadi would probably be gone as well. The market would be open all week, but she wanted to get to Tyre the next day and make the long trip to Shunem the following day.

"That is much too heavy for you to pull. Let me help." The man startled her.

Bina turned to face him. He appeared to be over sixty years old, a full gray beard and thinning hair to contrast his facial hair. Despite his age, his eyes were bright, and nearly the color of Palus' chocolate skin. One missing tooth off center accented his pleasant smile. She considered herself tall but he seemed six feet three or more inches tall, making her have to look up slightly to meet his eyes.

"I would appreciate that. I think I would wear out before getting back to the inn. However, I must stop at the cookware booth," Bina said.

"Would that be Gadi's booth?"

"Why, yes."

"His business is booming. I think he has sold about everything the first day. He credited that to a Shunammite Woman named Bina."

"Does he still have the same large bronze pot?"

"We will soon find out. Ready to start pulling?"

"Yes." Bina was surprised at the old man's strength.

"By the way, my name is Nathan. I live in Endor."

"We are of the same tribe." Bina didn't intend to reveal her name. That would happen at Gadi's stores.

They threaded through the narrow streets, stopping occasionally to rest. Several times their eyes met and they exchanged smiles.

Finally, Gadi's booth lay ahead. It was like Nathan said, Gadi's stores were bare, and only a few cups, a pitcher and hand utensils were all that remained. She spotted the pot and Gadi had made a crude sign that said SOLD. Bina was disappointed for she had money left to buy it, perhaps with some haggling with Gadi.

"Bina, I can't thank you enough for loaning me these certified weights. Next time I'll order more goods. Here are your weights back," Gadi said.

"Keep them. I have more. I wish I could have bought that pot," Bina said.

"The buyer is right here," Gadi said, pointing to Nathan.

"You bought the pot?" Bina asked.

"I bought it for you. I didn't mean to spy on you," Nathan said, picking up the heavy pot and wedging it between bags of seeds.

"But why?"

"I wanted to make sure you got it. I knew how bad you wanted it. Don't try to pay me for it," Nathan said.

"It must have been expensive. I need to compensate you for it."

"Please, no. All I ask is if there is an empty house in Shunem where I can stay."

"But what about your family?"

"My wife died two years ago and my son and daughter-in-law would prefer I move out."

"I am sorry, but yes there are a few empty houses in Shunem not far from where I live," Bina said.

"Would you mind if we travel together?" Nathan seemed to be holding his breath.

"It would be safer for both of us to travel together and the Lord will watch over us. Do you have a wagon and horse?" Bina asked.

"No. I just helped my family with buying and they will be leaving for Endor day after tomorrow," Nathan said.

"I'll be stopping at a friend's house in Tyre for the night. I know Nava will not mind putting you up. Her house is roomy."

When they arrived at the inn the Roman soldiers warned them of thieves between Sidon and Mount Carmel. They were glad that Bina would be traveling with Nathan but were concerned that Nathan was not a young man.

"We have an extra sword. Strap it on. Perhaps that will discourage thieves from attacking you," one of the soldiers said.

"But I don't know how to use a sword. I was too old to join Joram's host and at the upper age limit for Ahab's host, besides I certainly didn't want to be associated with Ahab anyway," Nathan said.

"No matter. Just seeing the sword may be enough." The soldier helped load Bina's sacks of seed onto her wagon. Nathan thought the sword didn't look at all daunting but not to offend the soldiers, he accepted the gesture with graciousness.

Bina's affection for Nathan was growing. She recognized his outstanding character, the way he dealt with the soldiers and most of all his kindness to her.

Early the next morning after breakfast she and Nathan pulled out of Sidon. The weather threatened to turn to the worse. Bina strapped a tarp across the exposed sides of the wagon to protect the bags of seeds from a certain rain. She thought perhaps the storm would discourage any thieves. They passed the village of Zarapheth in a driving rain and headed on toward Tyre. Bina and Nathan both had rain gear and kept reasonably dry except their heads.

"Did you see movement up ahead at the side of the road?" Nathan asked.

"I think so. Let's speed up," Bina said.

Before they could, three men rushed to the middle of the road, blocking it and spooking Bina's horse. Her horse reared on his hind legs and one of the men side stepped and grasped the horse's harness. Her horse turned his head and bit the man. One other man beat the horse mercilessly until he fell to his knees. The third man pulled Bina from her seat, causing her to fall into the mud. Nathan kicked one of the men in the teeth and pulled his sword.

"You're outnumbered old man," one of the men growled.

Nathan raised his sword at one man but another man beat him on the head from behind, downing him into the slimy road. He attempted to get up but was kicked down. Bina rose to her hands and knees.

"Please do not hurt us," she cried.

"Shut up!"

"Dear Lord, help us," she managed and limped toward Nathan who was trying to regain his feet.

Just then she heard the thunder of hooves coming from the direction of Tyre. In the driving rain she could see two soldiers, perhaps Roman, with their swords drawn.

They dismounted from their horses while the horses were still running. The thieves scattered, running for the cover where they had hidden. The soldiers chased them into the drenching rain.

After the thieves were gone, the soldiers returned to tend to Bina and Nathan. They helped them both up. Bina noticed one of the soldiers was older, but she judged both were seasoned fighters.

"Sir, you have a nasty gash on the back of your head," the older soldier examined Nathan's injury.

"I'll be alright. See about Bina."

"She's fine, standing right here."

"I thank the Lord who sent you to help us," Bina said.

"I wish I had your faith," the younger soldier said.

"The rain is letting up. It is only a few miles to Tyre. Are you able to go on?" The older soldier asked.

"Yes, we will stay at Bina's friend's house in Tyre," Nathan managed.

"Bina, take care of your father. He has a nasty cut." With their parting remark, they rode off in the direction of Sidon.

"You didn't know I was your father did you?" Nathan asked.

"No," Bina gave a wet smile.

Her horse had regained his feet and seemed okay. Bina figured any other animal would still be down. They wasted no time in moving on in case the thieves might try again. The rain had stopped and the road was sloppy, the wagon wheels cutting in the mud surface. Bina's horse still had no trouble despite the heavier load. She couldn't help but smile at the severe bite delivered to one of the thieves by her horse. Joram had done her a great service by giving the horses to her. Aside from their strength, they were as faithful as a pet.

Nava was waiting for them when they arrived. She gasped at their condition and immediately noted Nathan was hurt. He was hunched over, holding his head.

"Quick, Bina, help him in," Nava said, after they pulled their wagon and horse into the barn.

"This is Nathan. We met at the market. Thieves attacked us just two miles up the road. Thankfully, two Roman soldiers saved us."

"Let me tend to that cut," Nava said, and helped him to her kitchen.

"Nathan, I'm so sorry this happened to you. I should never have put you in danger," Bina said, laying her hand gently on his shoulder.

"Don't be sorry. I'm glad we are traveling together. Like you said, the Lord took care of us."

"In the form of my horse's good bite, your foot with that one thief's mouth and the two soldiers," Bina said, chuckling and taking a breath.

"You two will be okay. Mt. Carmel and your final stretch to Shunem afford wide open road and no place for thieves to hide along the way," Nava said.

"Are you able to travel on early in the morning?" Bina asked Nathan.

"Yes. A good night of rest and Nava's great dressing of my injury will see me through."

Nava's supplying them with dry clothes, preparation of a hardy evening meal and comfortable beds for them did wonders. After breakfast in the morning, the nightmare on the road seemed a distant memory. Bina set a definite month and day for her festival so Nava could be sure to come.

As they started out toward Mt. Carmel, the air was cool, crisp, having been washed clean by the previous day's rain. Bina enjoyed the fine weather and good company of Nathan. They made better time on the final leg to Shunem despite a loaded wagon. Going toward home always seemed faster than leaving home.

Palus spotted them as twilight moved in. He was glad, actually seeming relieved as his dark features always gave him away to Bina.

"What is wrong, Palus?" She asked after introducing Nathan and including a brief account of their journey.

"It's Abishag. I don't believe she will last another day." Bina left Palus, with Nathan's help, to unload the wagon, while she ran to Abishag's house. She knew Abishag must be critically ill as she wasn't on her porch. Bina rushed in and headed for her bedroom. The old woman brightened when she saw Bina.

"Oh, Bina. I'm so glad you're here. I'm not suffering from any disease. My old body is worn out. I can tell my time is very near."

"Don't talk like that," Bina said, tears flowing.

"I've have had a long and happy life. Did I ever tell you I was so thankful that Solomon didn't grant Adonijah his request to take me as his wife? He was not a good man and tried to take the throne that was rightfully Solomon's."

"Yes, you did, my dear. It was his undoing as you told me," Bina answered.

"That's putting it mildly." Abishag paused and laughed weakly and then continued.

"I have something I want to give you. I've kept it all these years. King David gave it to me just before he died. He signed it and made a personal gift to me. He called it The Shepherd's Psalm. He predicted it would give encouragement to all future generations."

Bina read the psalm out loud.

The Lord is my shepherd; I shall not want.

He maketh me to lie down in green pastures: he leadeth me beside the still waters.

He restoreth my soul: he leadeth me in the paths of righteousness for his name's sake.

Yea, though I walk through the valley of the shadow of death, I will fear no evil: for thou art with me; thy rod and thy staff they comfort me.

Thou preparest a table before me in the presence of mine enemies: thou anointest my head with oil; my cup runneth over.

Surely goodness and mercy shall follow me all the days of my life: and I will dwell in the house of the Lord forever.

Bina sat with Abishag through the night holding her hand. She knew the moment her spirit left her body for the old friend's body shook. Afterwards her hand lost its warmth. Bina shook with sobs until the sun cleared the hills running along the western slope of the Jordan Valley. Nathan and Palus arrived and Bina met them.

"She's gone," she uttered, failing to hold her voice steady, and then shed tears she didn't know she had left. Nathan pulled her into a gentle embrace and she wrapped him with her arms.

"I'm so sorry, My Lady," Palus said. Bina reached and grasped his hand.

"She wants to be buried here in Shunem and facing Jerusalem, where as a girl, she felt her life had meaning in the service of King David," Bina said.

All of Shunem knew of Abishag's long history and mourned thirty days, a practice going back to Moses when he died. Nathan encouraged Bina to concentrate on her festival plans. Palus had put in the crops using the seed Bina had bought at the market. She used special storage techniques to preserve the produce from the previous year. She had dug a sizeable storage area, with help from Palus, hauled blocks of ice during the winter from the frozen river

Kishon, used straw, and the storage cellar remained cold through the summer.

Abishag had instructed Bina to have her house and she talked Nathan into living there. As the festival time drew near, Nathan seemed sad one day as they were working together to set tables and readying her new cookware.

"What's wrong, Nathan?" Bina asked.

"A problem I can't overcome. I'd rather not talk about it," Nathan said, looking down.

"We're good friends. We can talk between us."

"Well, it concerns you." Nathan appeared embarrassed.

"Me? Have I offended you in some way?" Bina asked.

"You don't have an offending bone in your body."

"What a nice thing to say, but then what?" Bina stopped what she was doing. Nathan took a deep breath and touched his beard.

"I wish I were about forty years younger. I would . . ." He stopped, and then eyed the tables, putting them in a straighter line.

"You would what?"

"Ask you to be my wife," Nathan said, swallowed and looked away.

"Why Nathan, how sweet." She beamed her best smile, sincere indeed.

"I'm much too old for you. You would do better with a younger man." Bina could still see his darkened countenance.

"Need I remind you of Boaz and Ruth back during the time of the judges? Boaz was much older than Ruth." Bina observed a distinct improvement, his eyes sparkling, and his lips spreading into a smile.

"You mean?" Nathan left it unsaid.

"It isn't proper for the woman to take the first step here," Bina said.

"Will you be my wife?" Nathan asked and took both of her hands.

"Yes." She didn't hesitate. Nathan didn't hesitate either and pulled her into an embrace and kissed her tenderly.

Since Nathan was a widower, the betrothal period needed only to be thirty days. Nathan's parents were not present and Bina's parents were deceased, and with the blessings of an old Levite in Shunem, parties at the groom's house and formalities involving the bride's family as well were dispensed with. The feast of Shunem was perfect timing and Nava was so happy for Bina and served as her "family" member. Palus served as Nathan's friend and sent a gift to Bina which amounted to several date seeds that had sprouted.

"My Lady, you actually bought these seeds for me," he said to Bina.

"Yes, but your expert treatment and caring for those seeds so they sprouted were your doing. You knew to turn the seed to where the crevasse faced upward for easy of sprouting."

At the feast as everyone was at their places at the long tables, Nathan presented Bina with the silver betrothal ring and recited with great feeling.

"You are consecrated to me according to the law of Moses and Israel." With that said, he slipped the ring on her finger. All present cheered as Bina looked at the ring in its proper place, smiled and wrapped her arms around Nathan's neck as he drew her into a kiss.

*   *   *

Two years went by and crops were good. The seed Bina bought at the Sidon market exceeded her expectations. She, Nathan and Palus worked together and the produce was so plentiful that Bina distributed to the needy of Shunem. There were elderly widows, orphans, families with little land and even less farming implements or animals. Bina was the most prosperous person in Shunem and now, with Nathan, things were looking very good, but Nathan expressed what he perceived as a problem that Bina had not mentioned.

"I am sorry I have been unable to give you a child," he said, as they were sharing a meal one evening. Palus was in the barn caring for the two horses.

"We have each other. You have made me very happy." Bina reached over and grasped Nathan's hand.

"Thank you. As a young woman I'm sure you would like to have a son or daughter. The problem is I'm too old."

"Don't say that. It may be the Lord has closed my womb. It has happened to many in our history. There were

Sarah, Rachel, Hannah, maybe some others I've forgotten," Bina said.

"Yes, but the three you named finally had children," Nathan said.

"Do not fret about this, my husband. The Lord knows best," Bina said.

"You are truly a great woman, Bina. I wish I had a measure of your faith. Solomon wrote about a woman like you in the last of his proverbs a hundred years ago."

"Oh, I don't measure up to the virtuous woman he described."

"Of course you do. Don't say otherwise."

Bina thought about Solomon's last proverbs. The Virtuous Woman was praised by her husband and children. She cared for them tirelessly. Bina didn't let on, but she would like to have a child. However, she refused to complain. She was happy and the Lord had blessed her in so many ways she lost count.

*   *   *

Bina's home allowed her a view of those who journeyed through Shunem. The main road split the town and headed toward Mount Carmel and The Great Sea then along the valley of Jezreel and the Jordan River in the other direction. Many travelers seemed weary, and with Nathan's permission, she opened her doors and kitchen to those who appeared hungry and tired.

An older man, balding and with a beard, caught her eye. He was different than others who journeyed by their home. There was purpose in his trudge, his step labored, weary, but urgent and sure. She could tell from his countenance that his trip must have started quite early this day. He carried a long staff, wore a mantle that somehow conveyed a religious significance to her. She had recognized many people whom she knew were suffering from hunger or thirst or both. It was built into her abilities and gave her an urgency to respond to their needs. Quickly she conferred that to Nathan who agreed to her course of action. She darted out of the house and called to the traveler.

"Sir, please accept our offer. Stop and have something to eat," Bina said.

The man slowly turned at the sound of her voice. He centered his eyes on her, the curl of his lips barely detected in the center of his beard. Bina could see his smile as he turned and stepped toward her. She bowed gracefully, extending her hand toward her house and followed him two steps behind. Nathan met him at the door, greeting him, showing him to the kitchen as Bina gracefully side-stepped him while he sat down.

"I hope you like date bread. I bought date seeds from the Sidon market two years ago. Palus, our servant, planted the seeds at that time and they flourished." Bina placed a plate in front of the traveler. He said a prayer of thanks and took a bite.

"This is delicious. I have not tasted bread such as this before," he said, following with water and added, "The water is cold and pure, I see."

"From a nearby spring. The water is cool year around," Nathan said.

Bina enjoyed seeing the traveler eat his fill. She restrained her curiosity as to his identity, not wanting to pry into his business. He didn't stay long after eating.

"Our home is open to you. Please stop here on your journeys through Shunem," Bina said.

"I thank you for your kindness. I will have a servant with me later."

"He is welcome too, always."

The traveler left and Bina thought he had new energy as he proceeded on. It was two weeks before he came back from the direction of Mount Carmel. His return trip toward Mount Carmel was in two weeks again. He stopped each time, taking advantage of Bina and Nathan's hospitality. Each time he stopped and after Bina observed his actions and heard his brief comments she realized this was a holy man of God. She had seen a sanctuary at Mount Carmel so that confirmed it in her mind. She expressed her perception to Nathan.

"My husband, the traveler must be a holy man of God who comes by here on a regular basis. We have an unfinished room upstairs. Let us prepare it and furnish it with a bed, a table, a stool and a candlestick. He brought a servant last trip so we can provide him a bed too."

"I have noticed him carrying parchments so the table and candlestick are appropriate," Nathan said.

Bina, Nathan and Palus labored for two days to enclose the upper level of their house and construct an exterior stairs to the room. The room was furnished and Bina added a date palm she had started in a wooden tub. It reached three feet and she felt it brightened an otherwise dull looking room and would remind the traveler of her date bread. The candlesticks were cast from copper by a resident of Shunem who was skilled in metal work.

The traveler had his servant with him and Bina ran to meet them while they were still over a hundred feet away.

"Please, the two of you, we have made a room on the upper level for you to rest and sleep. Follow me."

"You are most kind. I am Gehazi. Master Elisha and I will spend the night as the day is already far spent."

"You are Elisha? Forgive me for my rashness. I knew you were a holy man of God but I had no idea you were Elisha," Bina said and dropped to her knees, bowing her head.

"Please, daughter of Issachar, stand up. I am just a mortal man like others," Elisha said.

"You are not like other men. Are you not clothed with Elijah's mantle? You have performed miracles, and I am told Elijah passed his powers on to you. We are deeply honored to meet you and have you under our roof," Bina said, slowly standing.

"You and your family have been most hospitable to us," Elisha said.

"I will bring you food," Bina said and entered her house as Elisha and Gehazi climbed the stairs. She couldn't restrain her excitement as she revealed the traveler's identity to Nathan and Palus.

The third time Elisha and Gehazi stopped and stayed in the room Bina, Nathan and Palus had built, Gehazi came down from their room and delivered a message from Elisha to Bina.

"My Lady, Elisha would like to see you." Bina could not imagine why Elisha would want to see her. She followed Gehazi up the stairs and stood just inside the room's door. On this meeting Elisha chose to talk to her through Gehazi. Bina perceived it could be because of the seriousness of his request.

"Behold, you have been careful for us with all this care; what is to be done for you? Would you want me to speak for you to King Joram or to the captain of the host?"

"I dwell among mine own people," Bina answered without hesitation. She noted Elisha and Gehazi remained speechless, apparently surprised she hadn't asked for some exalted position in the king's court for Nathan or some other advantage for her family. She knew Nathan would approve of her answer and Palus was content to be with her and Nathan as well. Truly, she was content to be among her people in Shumen, and remain in the tribe of Issachar, the land of inheritance given by God to Jacob and Leah's fifth son. She stepped out the door and started down the steps when she overheard Elisha and Gehazi's reaction to her answer.

"What then is to be done for her?" Elisha asked Gehazi. Bina stopped on the second step from the top. Humbleness swept over her at Elisha's gratitude toward her. She didn't consider her "care" for Elisha and Gehazi to be any greater than what she'd done for the people of Shunem. Of course she'd rendered help to Abishag in her old age, she'd helped many needy people in Shunem, there was the couple on the road to Tyre, and also helped Gadi learn the lesson of honesty in Sidon's market. The Lord had granted her the means to do that. She was only putting the blessings of the Lord to work for others. Bina listened intently to Gehazi's answer.

"Verily she hath no child, and her husband is old." Bina wondered what Gehazi was implying by that answer. Was he perceptive about what lay in her heart? What she hadn't revealed to anyone? It was fortunate she didn't descend farther than the second step from the top because Elisha emphatically ordered Gehazi to, "Call her!"

She took the two steps back to the door of their room and stood there without entering. Elisha spoke immediately at her appearance.

"About this set time according to the time of life you shall embrace a son."

"Nay, my lord, man of God, do not lie to your handmaid," Bina said and regret clutched her like one of Shunem's past and severe winters. How dare she speak to the great prophet Elisha in such a way, but her and Nathan had tried to start a family since they married about three years ago. She had conceded, but without complaint, that a combination of Nathan's age and the Lord possibly closing her womb was the reason for her failure to conceive.

She knew when the conception happened. The great prophet Elisha showed just how great he was. Bina waited patiently for his next appearance in Shunem. When he and Gehazi came, she didn't wait until they took the stairs to their room. She ran to meet them before they reached their home.

"Oh, great prophet. I have asked God to forgive me and now I am asking you to forgive my terrible words to you. It is as you said. I am with child."

"There is no need to ask my forgiveness. It is understandable for your words as you have been unable to conceive after these three years," Elisha said.

"I know of your past miracles and it is inexcusable for me to call you a liar." Bina bowed her head.

"I only require some of your good date bread and that cool spring water for myself and Gehazi."

"It is fresh baked and I will bring it to you," Bina said.

The months passed and Bina wondered if she should travel to Tyre and seek out the midwife who tended to the couple she had helped during her journey to Sidon. She mentioned it to Nathan and Palus one evening. Nathan had been overprotective, in her opinion, due to her condition.

"No need to travel to Tyre. I helped my wife in the delivery of our son," Nathan said.

"My Lady, the Ethiopian women needed some help in their deliveries and I learned much from my mother and sisters as they served as midwives for the women of our country," Palus said.

Bina was uncertain about the well-meaning offers of her husband and servant. During her eighth month she had a surprise visit from her good friend, Nava, who revealed that Elisha had sent Gehazi to Tyre on one of his trips to Mount Carmel. Gehazi had told Nava when Bina's baby was due. With all due respects to Nathan and Palus, Bina was relieved to have Nava's help during delivery.

The baby was due in the hottest part of the summer. Bina told everyone she wanted the boy born under a pine tree near the spring. The house was hot and the tree offered shade and the spring had a coldness that contributed a little to comfort from the heat. There was another reason too, but she wouldn't reveal that just yet. Nava had everything ready as Bina's contractions started. They shortened in duration quickly and Bina told the men to stay at a distance until the boy came into the world. The delivery went well and Nava made an observation.

"Bina, you were like the Jewish women when our people were in Egypt and Moses was born. That was nearly nine hundred years ago. They delivered their babies rather quickly."

Bina looked at her newborn and tears streamed down her cheeks. She looked at Nava who motioned for Nathan and Palus. As all three of them took turns holding the baby boy and then returned the precious little bundle back to Bina, she revealed the final reason for having the baby born under the pine tree.

"His name is Oren."

"What a perfect name. It means pine tree," Palus said.

"Now you know the real reason I wanted him born here. I can stand the heat of summer. The heat was only of secondary importance," Bina said.

"Our lives are going to change around here," Nathan said. Bina's tears began again.

"The Lord has truly blessed us with our new arrival. Why did I ever doubt Elisha? I can't wait for him to stop by next time."

It was two weeks when Elisha and Gehazi stopped at Bina's. Nathan saw them and beckoned they enter the house before going upstairs to their room. Bina was just finished nursing Oren. Elisha and Gehazi approached, smiling. Elisha sat down beside mother and child.

"His name is Oren. I gave birth to him out under our pine tree."

"How appropriate," Elisha said.

Elisha reached his hand toward the baby. Oren extended his hand toward Elisha and circled his small hand around Elisha's finger and smiled at the old prophet.

"That is amazing. I don't know how soon a newborn would do that but it seems too early," Bina said.

"This is the child Elisha promised you. I think the boy somehow recognizes that Elisha is responsible for him being in this world as promised," Gehazi said.

"Or perhaps the child knows it was you who suggested my desire for a child in the first place. See, he is also smiling at you," Bina said.

"You are most kind, My Lady," Gehazi said, and did a slight bow of reverence to her.

"Oren is in good hands. We will retire to our room. We must get an early start in the morning for Mount Carmel. A feast day of the Lord's is in a few days," Elisha said.

*   *   *

The field next to their house was ripe for harvesting. Nathan hired young men as reapers to help. Oren, being five years old, begged Bina that he might go see his father while the reaping proceeded. Bina cautioned Oren to stay in the shade for the sun was beaming down relentlessly. Nathan and the reapers wore turbans that covered the back of their necks. Bina provided the same protection for Oren.

Bina saw in the far end of the field that Oren had removed his turban. She made out that he spoke to Nathan and was holding his head. Nathan spoke to one of the reapers and he picked Oren up and ran toward the house. Bina met them and Oren said, "Mother, my head, my head."

She took Oren from the reaper and went into the house. She sat down, took Oren onto her knees and held him. He continued to complain about his head hurting. Bina felt of his forehead. It was hot and the child closed his eyes, his breathing labored. He lapsed into unconsciousness.

"Oh, Oren," Bina cried. She held him, hugged him and drew his head close to her, putting her hand gently around him. She didn't know what to do after wetting a cloth with cold spring water and holding it against his head which was still hot. She rocked and knew his life was threatened by what she thought was a sun stroke. She shook with sobs and at noon his soul left his body so that he died.

Bina took Oren up the stairs on the outside of the house, entered Elisha's room and laid him on Elisha's bed. She left the room and shut the door behind her. She went out to the field and called Nathan to ask him to send Palus to get their two horses ready.

"Send me Palus that he may fetch our two horses that we may go to Elisha and come again," Bina said.

"Why? It is neither new moon nor Sabbath."

"It shall be well," Bina said. She had faith in the man of God, and then turned to Palus. "Saddle our horses and take us forward quickly to Mount Carmel. Do not slow down on my account unless I tell you."

Bina's war horses gobbled the sixteen miles quickly, Palus letting his horse run at will. Both horses seemed to sense Bina's urgency as she patted her horse's flank. She was relieved when she saw Elisha ahead. Elisha's servant ran to meet them. When Gehazi met them, Bina jumped off her horse as her and Palus pulled up in a cloud of dust.

"Is it well with you, your husband and the child?" Gehazi asked.

"It is well," Bina answered.

She fell before Elisha and grabbed his feet. Gehazi came near to push her away.

"Let her alone. Her soul is vexed within her; and the Lord has hidden the reason for her suffering and not told me," Elisha said. Gehazi then retreated.

"Did I desire a son of my lord? Did I not say do not deceive me?" Bina uttered, her voice betraying her agony.

Elisha turned to Gehazi and said, "Gird up your loins and take my staff in your hand and go. Do not salute any man you might meet and if any salute you, do not return the greetings. Lay my staff on the face of the child."

Palus helped Gehazi up to sit behind him and Palus spurred the horse away back to Shunem. After they were gone, Bina felt compelled to address Elisha for she had faith that he was the only one who would do what God deemed right and good.

"As the Lord lives and as you live, Oh man of God, I will not leave you."

She motioned to Elisha, indicating for him to climb up behind her as she mounted. Elisha didn't hesitate and got on behind her. She pushed her mount and he didn't hesitate to take his passengers at top speed back to Shunem. Bina told herself inwardly that everything truly is well with Elisha going back with her.

They were not far behind Palus and Gehazi for as they approached the house, Gehazi was coming down the stairs.

"The child has not awakened," Gehazi said. Elisha got down from the horse and ascended the steps to his room, shutting the door behind him. Gehazi told Bina what she already knew.

"Your son is dead, My Lady."

"Elisha is here. Everything will be all right."

Nathan and Palus both hugged her and that almost caused her to break down.

They all waited below. Gehazi encouraged them and expounded what he witnessed since being a servant to Elisha. Bina remained calm but as the time approached an hour, she battled with herself concerning her faith, and then chastised herself for the sinful doubt that lurked over her head like a severe storm cloud threatening to strike.

Bina couldn't sit still in the house. She had made the trip outside five times in the past hour. She remained outside on the last trip. Gehazi ascended the steps and entered their room. Another ten minutes passed as Bina continued to say a silent prayer.

Gehazi appeared at the upper room's door.

"My lady, Elisha would like for you to come up."

Bina stepped lively, bounding up the steps, knowing this summons was a good sign. Gehazi stepped aside allowing her to enter the room. Elisha extended his arm toward her son.

"Take up your son."

Bina drew a quick breath and fell at Elisha's feet.

"My dear and holy prophet. Again, I ask your forgiveness and ask God to forgive my improper addressing of you when Oren died.

"Your remarks were understandable and what you said was true. At that time your child indeed was gone," Elisha said.

"You are most gracious and have granted me leniency I do not deserve," Bina said and took her son into her arms. Tears spilled down her cheeks as she hugged Oren, pressing his face into her bosom. At the door she turned and looked at Elisha.

"I thank the Lord that you came into my life and granted me this most unspeakable gift."

"My Lady, it is God who has looked favorably on you. Your reputation is widespread. You think of others and that is the mark of a godly person: to be of service to others."

"Your kind words are most gracious. I pray I can live up to them."

* * *

A year later Elisha and Gehazi stopped on their way to Mount Carmel and came directly to the living quarters instead of going to their upper room. Bina thought it odd and knew right away that the old prophet had something important to say. It was evening and she, Nathan, Palus and Oren had just finished their evening meal. Bina was in the process of cleaning up.

"Please sit down, Holy Prophet and Gehazi. We are most honored to have you under our roof as always," Bina said.

"You must all go and sojourn wheresoever you can for the Lord hath called for a famine; and it shall come upon the land seven years."

Bina wasn't too surprised as they experienced poor crops and she wasted no time. She thanked Elisha and he left.

"Evidence of the approaching famine by the prophet is verified by our poor harvest that has just passed," Palus said.

"Yes. Palus I want you to carry the prophet's message throughout Shunem this evening. Everyone here knows Elisha and what he has done these past several years. They will believe God's message about the coming famine," Bina said.

"As you wish, My Lady. You always have other's welfare at heart," Palus replied, and then left.

They worked into the night methodically gathering what they felt was essentials. Bina judged they should go into the land of the Philistines. This was met with objections from both Nathan and Palus.

"The Philistines are enemies of Israel. They made their camp right here in Shunem and launched their attack from here to Mount Gilboa and killed King Saul. That was only about a hundred and fifty years ago," Nathan said.

"If I may but speak, My Lady. During the time of your judges did not Samson kill thousands of Philistines?" Palus asked.

"Both of you recollect our history correctly. I do not remember hearing of the Philistines mistreating anyone in Shunem when they were here. Of course all our young men were in Saul's army, not here. The Philistine warrior Goliath was defeated by King David and that put the fear into them. More recently it was the Syrians who killed King Ahab, not the Philistines. For now the hostilities between Israel and Philistia have ceased," Bina said.

"Nevertheless, memories of past conflicts probably remain intact," Nathan said.

"My husband, the land of the Philistines lies to our south along the Great Sea and I doubt the famine will reach that far," Bina said.

"Your judgment has always been as sound as a millstone, Bina," Nathan said.

"Thank you. We will journey south to Taanach. There is a pass through the mountains of Gilboa there. We will be able to take it and finish our trek to Philistia. Their land is about eighty miles from here as the raven flies," Bina said.

"Mother I want to help with the packing," Oren said, tugging at Bina's long garment.

"Of course, Oren. Your father needs help. He will show you what kitchen utensils to take to our wagon. We all have to pitch in."

The four of them loaded the wagon with water, kitchen items, food that wouldn't spoil, clothing, spare parts for the wagon, and feed for their two horses. A canvas wrapped tightly would serve as protection at night should they encounter bad weather. Bina took the gold she had left and stashed it in the compartment under the wagon's bed. Nathan, Palus and Oren were finishing packing as Bina sat down in the kitchen and looked at the cupboards which were bare. It saddened her to leave home, the place she held so dear. Others in Shunem must feel the same way.

Elisha appeared while she was alone. He seemed to sense her disturbance at having to leave.

"You will be able to return in seven years after the famine is over," he said.

"Do you read minds too, my dear prophet?"

Elisha laughed, something Bina hadn't remember him doing before.

"Call it common sense and not a mind reading gift. The Lord sometimes allows me that ability but not at this instant."

Bina smiled and Elisha asked her to stand up. Puzzled, Bina got up and faced Elisha. Beneath that beard and in those eyes there shown a deep respect as he stared at her.

"Besides providing you and your husband the ability to have a child, I want to impart a gift to you," he said, and uncharacteristic of him, he placed his hands on her shoulders.

"But you have given me more than I could ever want," Bina said, looking down and bowing slightly. His hands radiated a special feeling on her shoulders. Something coursed through her body. She gasped and then sighed, closing her eyes, drinking in the wonderful sensation.

"This will be something you can give to others, two people to be exact," he said.

"My dear prophet, I felt something enter my body, a wonderful feeling, warm, beneficial."

"I have imparted to you the ability to heal others. It is limited to two persons of your choosing. You can touch them as I am touching you. You must then recite the prayer in these words. 'Dear Lord, heal this poor soul of their disease, Amen.' If these persons are unworthy to be healed then it will not happen so choose wisely," Elisha said, and then removed his hands.

"Oh, prophet I am not worthy of such a gift," Bina said, bowing her head in reverence.

"You are worthy and I know you will choose those two persons wisely. I will take my leave of you so you can finish preparing for your trip. I overheard you have decided to go to Philistia. That is a wise choice. The famine will not reach to the southern coast of the Great Sea," Elisha said, and then left to return to the upper room.

Nathan entered the kitchen and nodded respectfully to Elisha in passing.

"Did I hear the prophet right? Did he give you the ability to heal two persons?"

"Yes, isn't wonderful?"

"Bina, promise me one thing. I am old and I don't want you to use your gift to extend my life."

"But my husband I do not want to lose you. If I can give you more years then. . .,"

"No, Bina. Use your gift for a couple of persons who are very sick and are younger. I am sure Elisha would want you to do that."

Bina sighed. She knew Nathan was right but didn't look forward to him going to be with the Lord before her if that was the case.

The next morning they left just after the night gave way to the dawn. Bina noticed others leaving toward the south country in the Jordan Valley and she hoped they were making the right choice. No travelers seemed to be going her way, however. She looked toward Mount Carmel and saw Elisha and Gehazi had just left as well.

They found the pass through the Gilboa mountain range and traveled south to Taanach. At less than ten miles they arrived in Taanach late morning. As they stopped for a break in their travels, Bina thought of the history of the area. She wished she had known the female judge, Deborah, and her army leader Barak, but most of all the brave woman, Jael, who drove a tent peg through the Canaanite army captain, Sisera's temples. Bina shuddered at that image but admired Jael for her bravery.

"Bina, I believe we can make the Plain of Sharon along the coast of the Great Sea before nightfall," Nathan said.

"Yes, we can find a small village to stay at or just camp near the sea. I believe our horses will like the sea foaming around their hooves," Bina answered.

"My Lady, depending on the lay of the land we should make the southern border of the tribe of Dan's land tomorrow evening," Palus added.

"That will put us into the land of the Philistines the following day," Bina observed.

"At that point we will have to decide where we can settle, either Ashdod on the river, Ashkelon on the sea coast, Gaza farther south or Gath where the Philistine king is," Nathan said.

"Well, the king, if we get to see him, will know if there are any abandoned homesteads. After all, we are homeless and have very little money to buy a place to live," Bina said.

"What are we to do if the king does not know of a place for us?" Nathan asked.

"Have faith, my husband. I have a plan."

"Your name means wise and intelligent. It is certainly a proper name for you," Nathan said.

"I concur," Palus added.

"I thank both of you," Bina said, feeling her face heat up.

As they approached Gath, the way sloped upward toward the great walled city. Bina thought of David seeking refuge here when King Saul sought him. Later David had destroyed the city. Then Rehoboam had restored the city less than a hundred years ago. Would the Philistine king remember that David had killed Goliath near here? Would he remember David seeking protection here and then turning on them some forty years later? Hopefully, he would remember Rehoboam rebuilding the city.

As they approached the city, Bina noticed the crops in the surrounding area were unhealthy, not producing as they should. Perhaps her plan, if it worked, would win the heart of the Philistine king. They stood before the gate at midday. A man stood there opening the large gate as visitors or residents approached. Then he spotted them and held out his hand signaling them to stop.

"I do not recognize you. Where are you from?"

"We come from Shunem, located in the land allotted to the tribe of Issachar," Bina answered, knowing the truth was the best policy.

"Israelites. You came to spy out our land. You are our enemies," the man said, his forehead furrowing.

"Nay, there is a famine in our land. We need a place to live. Our prophet says it will last seven years," Bina answered.

"You may not enter." The man crossed his arms and stepped in front of them.

"What seems to be the problem here?" A soldier decked out in helmet, metal shoulder pads, strapped sword, and girdle of metal mesh.

"These Israelites are from Shunem, come to spy on our defenses," the gate man answered.

"Shunem? Our army encamped there and defeated the Israelites, killing their king years gone by. No one in Shunem caused us any trouble. You may pass," the soldier said, waving his hand.

"Thank you," Nathan said.

"If I may sir, we would like to see the king," Bina asked.

"Whatever for?" the soldier asked.

"I noticed your crops are failing. I have knowledge of farming and can help," Bina said.

"It is true, My Lady has grown enough before the famine to feed all of Shunem," Palus added.

"Follow me." The soldier led them into the heart of the city.

They followed him, their horses' hooves clopping on the hard and dusty ground. The king's palace, easily visible in the distance, dwarfed the surrounding shops and residences. Soldiers, stationed at the top of the wide steps, snapped to a rigid posture as Bina, Nathan and Palus got down from their wagon. Bina held Oren's hand. The soldier signaled a nearby guard to secure their wagon, and another soldier to precede them and tell the king of their visitors.

Bina admired the marble floors, but was disheartened by the wood, stone, iron, copper, silver and gold images lining the walls. Nathan, Palus and Oren craned their necks as well. Surrounding the four of them were soldiers decked with their swords, shields, gloved hands, armor and everything else they needed for battle and protection. A large ornate door reaching to the ceiling far above them slowly opened. A red carpet extended to a throne where sat the king.

Bina gasped as she took in, first the crown adorned with jewels, rubies, emeralds, sapphires, diamonds and other precious stones she didn't recognize. He had red, gold and green garments from neck to ankles. His eyes, dark and foreboding, gazed from Oren, Palus, Nathan and then settled on her and stayed. He smiled and took a deep breath.

"What does the lovely woman from Shunem have to offer that is so valuable that she took this chance to seek me out? I am Achish the fifth, after the first king to carry that name over a hundred and sixty years ago, my great-great-grandfather."

"Oh, King, I have seed from Egypt and farming knowledge that will help improve your crops," Bina answered.

"It is only because our history says your small village of Shunem did not rise up to resist our host, but of course your men of fighting age were with your king Saul. Nevertheless, I give you audience. There is a house near our stunted and pathetic attempt at farming and just outside of the city where you can stay. There should be a difference in two years in your farming."

"Thank you, O King. Your trust is most gracious." Bina bowed, but not with worship in mind.

The king added, "I find you a most wise and intelligent woman, a most trustworthy lady. I am never wrong in my snap judgment of character; else I would not be king."

"I will strive to live up to your judgment, O King."

*   *   *

The soldier who gained their access to the king led them to the farm with the stunted crops. He informed them the king would supply them with food and water. They would be on their own to repair the implements. However, the king did furnish three of his finest horses from the army's pastures.

When Bina saw the size of the fields, the condition of the ploughs and other implements, her heart sank.

"Nathan, Palus, we are going to need repair parts, tools, barn and underground storage improvement, all this before planting and ground preparation season."

"That is a tall order. The king may not give us money to buy what we need to get going. He has already given us horses, land and a house," Nathan said.

"My Lady, the king is expecting great things from you, from all of us. Do you think we can deliver, because it seems he expects you to lead us?" Palus asked.

"Yes, we can if we have to work through the daylight hours of the sundial and by the light of the moon. I have some gold left. It will be enough since the king is supplying our food," Bina said.

"You are always positive," Nathan and Palus echoed.

The city of Gath had the necessary parts for the dilapidated ploughs, tools and rough hewn lumber to make the improvements needed. Bina was relieved that the cost didn't deplete her gold band reserves. The whole family pitched in and repaired the farming implements and improved the barn and storage structures. They worked through the winter months, it taking much energy to get ready for planting in the spring. As that time arrived, Bina realized their labor would be even more demanding than what had been accomplished during the winter. She worried that it was taking its toll on Nathan.

The king's horses were strong but took training to get them used to pulling the ploughs. Palus seemed tireless in his efforts but was successful in getting the horses trained for something other than fearlessly carrying a soldier into battle.

With the soil finally worked into a fine texture, Bina applied the technique of crop rotation, planting barley where wheat grew the previous season. She did the same for corn, rye, even a small stand of dates.

By the end of their first years' growing season, the fields of grain were much improved and at the end of their second year king Achish inspected the crops and highly praised their efforts. He sent the surrounding cities' farmers to Bina so she could instruct them. Horsemen were sent to Gaza for the superior seed that Egyptian merchant boats had brought to the Great Sea port. All of Philistia benefitted from Bina's wisdom so that the Philistine plain thrived on the farmlands where once stood straggly crops.

During the third year Nathan was unable to help them. Old age was getting to him. His legs were weak, his stamina gone. He was failing fast and once again he forbid Bina to use one of her two individual healing gifts.

"Don't leave me, my husband," she said, as she sat by his bed on what would be his final night. Tears gushed down her cheeks as he muttered.

"Please speak my name, Bina."

"Nathan, I love you." She grasped his hand. He smiled, lifted his free hand to her cheek to brush away her tears, smiled again and then his hand dropped, his body shuddered briefly and he closed his eyes. Bina knew his spirit left his body with that final movement.

Many tears were shed that night by Bina, Palus and Oren. Their weeping was quiet as their supply of tears was not depleted.

For several days Bina didn't feel like working, but Palus admonished her that Nathan would want her to carry on. She admired Palus for his own wisdom. Without Nathan's help their work would be more difficult. The king recognized their plight and allowed the soldier who admitted them to Gath to help them. They finally learned his name was Flavius. He was strong, a fast learner and took orders from Bina without worrying that she was a woman and an Israelite at that.

During the fourth year King Achish invited Bina, Palus and Oren to the palace. It was the first time they had been there since their arrival. The king smiled and motioned for them to sit at the long, ornate table where he took his meals.

"I have wanted to express my gratitude for all you have done for us. You have not let our past histories hamper you," Achish said.

"I have always wanted our two nations to be at peace," Bina said.

"As have I. Our mutual history has been a stormy one. We killed King Saul, and your king David killed Goliath and David's men killed Goliath's brothers. David took this city more than once I believe. We took the ark of your God during one early battle we won, but your God caused us to suffer. We returned the ark according to the instructions of our priests and diviners. My Lady Bina, you have gone a long way in bringing us peace. Perhaps hostilities will flare up again but for now there is peace and I will do my best to keep it that way."

"I am glad to hear that, O, King."

They continued to talk of past history and what they hoped for the future. Bina admired this king and felt as long as he was king there would be peace. She remembered that this king's ancestor gave David refuge when he was on the run from Saul. By mere coincidence, during their talking, this King Achish mentioned that bit of history and how over a hundred and sixty years ago David and King Achish enjoyed a close relationship.

*　　*　　*

It was the sixth year since Bina and her household had resided in the Philistine's land, when Flavius returned after a brief trip to Gath.

"The king has stricken ill. The physicians do not know why. I am afraid he is going to die."

Bina had grown to trust King Achish to keep peace with Israel. Many lives would be saved on both sides. Elisha had imparted a gift of healing for two people to her. He had also prophesied that she would have the wisdom to choose those two people. Perhaps she shouldn't regard it as prophecy on Elisha's part, but rather continue to praise God for giving her wisdom and intelligence. Did that include the ability to make decisions that benefitted others? Dear Nathan and Palus expressed many times that judgment of her. King Achish would be the first of her two healings. She revealed her gift to Flavius and he wasted no time in taking her to Gath. The king's guard had come to trust her more and more as he served her on the farm and observed her actions and speech. They rode with haste to the city, bounded up the steps to the palace and hurried to the king's bedchamber. Flavius approached the king's bed and waved off the two physicians.

"O, King, Bina has something to tell you."

"I must beg your forgiveness for my inability to stand as a courtesy in the presence of such an esteemed woman," the king said. His voice was weak and Bina could hear a wheezing that slurred his speech. His face was pale; beads of perspiration dotted his face which had an unhealthy pallor.

"Dear King. Our prophet, Elisha, after foretelling of the approaching seven years of famine in our land, gave me a gift. It was the ability to heal two people of my choice. I have not yet used that gift. To the benefit of yourself, your nation and Israel too, I believe it would do well that I heal you," Bina said. She didn't approach the king, but waited on his response.

"I find you an honest lady. Please help me. I hope your judgment of my making a difference is true. I do not feel it is a king's weakness to feel humbled by your assessment of my worth." He extended his arms, the movement slow and shaky, toward Bina.

She took his hands briefly and then released them and moved her hands to rest on the king's shoulders just as Elisha had shown her. She took a deep breath, closing her eyes.

"Dear Lord, heal this poor soul of their disease, Amen."

The king drew a sudden, deep breath, his eyes darting from Bina's hands on his shoulders, to her face. He felt his cheeks and examined his own hands. His face was consumed by a broad smile.

"I am truly healed. It was so sudden. May I add that I hope you will stay here always?"

"I greatly desire to return to Shunem when the famine is over. That will be next year," Bina said.

"I can understand your roots are in Shunem. I would not be surprised if your character is praised in your manuscripts down through the centuries," Achish said.

"Is the king also a prophet?" Bina asked, smiling.

"I guess we will never know. It will be a sad day when you leave our country and journey back to yours."

"It will be a sad parting for me too. I will treasure knowing you and Flavius along with so many of your farmers," Bina said.

"I hope you still have your home in Shunem. Is there anyone who can help you if your home is occupied?"

"The Lord will provide for me."

As the year passed, Bina hoped her home wasn't occupied. She also wondered how she and Oren would care for their property by themselves. Yes, the Lord must provide. Although she had not mentioned it to Palus yet, she intended to give him his freedom so he could return to Ethiopia. The trip wouldn't be so long from Philistia for him. She knew he would probably want to stay on with her and Oren. It would be another sad parting, but she intended to persuade him to return to his homeland. It would not be the year of Jubilee for him as provided under the Mosaic

Law, but would the Lord object if Palus was set free before that time? Again, this would require delving into the law for its fine points and asking the Lord for guidance. Would Elisha still be around so she could ask him if need be?

Bina always kept Moses' writings with her and that included her present trip to Philistia. After Palus and Oren were asleep, and Flavius back in Gath in the service of the king, she went to the back room, lit a candle and sat down at the lone table. She unfurled the sacred manuscripts. Moses received God's law and she finally found and read the law concerning servants. The law was very specific in the case of an Israelite servant. Details concerning the year of Jubilee and an Israelite servant redeeming themselves before the jubilee year involved the servant paying the master money based on how many years served and how many years remained until the jubilee year. For foreign servants they could be kept for life and if they outlived their master then the master's children could inherit them.

No money was involved except the servant's purchase price.

If she knew Palus, she figured he would want to remain with her. She would like that but she wanted him to return to whatever family he had left. Her parents had purchased Palus when she was twelve. They all grew fond of him and Bina had the benefit of his invaluable help in the past, what nineteen years? She was now one and thirty. A week before the seven years famine should be up in Israel she breached the subject with Palus one evening.

"Palus, I want to set you free. You have been a faithful servant for our family these past nineteen years."

"No, My Lady. I will remain with you," Palus answered. Bina knew she would have a battle on her hands from his stern voice.

"You have family in Ethiopia, don't you?"

"Yes, two younger sisters whom I presume are still living. Our parents had died leaving us nothing. With no hope of work, I gladly provided money by talking them into selling me on the slave market. I count it lucky to be bought by your family."

"I have been more than happy with your loyal service. The trip from here to your homeland will be shorter and I will let you take one of the horses King Achish gave us."

"I often think of my two sisters but I will not let you and Oren make the trip alone back to Shunem. Forgive me from speaking improperly as a servant but I feel strongly about this," Palus said.

Bina sighed. Somehow, she needed to perform a final act of kindness to him, a small consolation to all he had done for her, Nathan and Oren. Two days later King Achish arrived escorted with twenty soldiers. Flavius was one of therm.

"I am honored by your send off, O, King," Bina said, standing in front of their dwelling place. The king with his accompanying soldiers was a formidable sight with their soldier attire and the horses, some of them snorting. The king dismounted from his white stallion, the saddle adorned with the Philistine's crest. Bina wondered if the gold trim was pure gold.

"I wish I could persuade you to stay, but I understand your desire to return to your homeland," King Achish said.

"O, King, if I may speak. My Lady insists on setting me free to return to my family in Ethiopia and then her and her son return to Israel alone. I fear for her safety," Palus said.

"Never fear, Palus. I am allowing Flavius here to return to his native land of Greece. He can go with My Lady, Bina, if she is agreeable," the king said, looking at Bina expectantly.

"I would be grateful of Flavius' company, but the Lord has always taken care of me. Perhaps this is his way of caring for me in the form of Flavius going with me and Oren," Bina said, bowing slightly and closing her eyes.

"Good, then it is settled. Words cannot express my country's appreciation for you instructing us on farming. I'll always remember you each time I view the lush farmlands and full grain bins as well as bringing me back from the brink of death."

"May I leave the two horses I brought with me in your care? They are old now and deserve to finish their days in a quiet pasture. King Joram gave them to me several years ago," Bina asked.

"But of course. Could you use another horse?" the king asked.

"Palus will take one back to Ethiopia. That leaves me two which is enough to work our land."

"Your son may like to have one for riding," the king commented. Bina saw Oren's eyes light up.

"Please, Mother. I want a horse of my own," Oren said, tugging on her sleeve.

"We have already imposed on the king enough."

"My Lady, our country has thousands of horses and it is small payment for all you have done for us."

"I see I am outvoted." Bina smiled at Oren and the king. He had brought a horse with no rider. Bina truly didn't mind the assertiveness of the king. She recognized that as the mark of a great leader.

King Achish grasped Bina's hands firmly, said a few more endearing words and left. Flavius remained with a rolled blanket secured over his horse's rump, presumably with his meager belongings. Bina watched the king and his soldiers ride briskly away. She had grown fond of the king. His personality was not one of haughtiness or arrogance like some may expect from a king. His subjects were happy, just like she had read about how Israel felt when Solomon was king. It was said that the queen of Sheba recognized that when she visited Solomon to verify what she heard of him.

The day Bina planned to leave arrived. It was going to be a painful goodbye to Palus. The look on his face said it all; as she was sure her expression mirrored his. She took his hands as he stood beside the saddled horse. His belongings equaled Flavius' blanket roll. He drew a deep breath, staring down at his and her hands intertwined.

"Our lives have been filled with painful goodbyes. I do not want to enumerate them," Bina said.

"It does not have to be, My Lady," Palus answered.

"I have set you free. Please, do not feel you need to use the title, 'My Lady', now." Bina smiled, but she felt an element of sadness touch her face.

"Well, if I may be so bold as to say I like using the title and inform you it carries more than just a servant speaking to his master. Although our parting carries much pain, I look forward to seeing my sisters again."

"I want you to take these. You will probably need them for your trip." Bina handed Palus three large gold bands and a few small ones.

"Oh, I cannot take these."

"Yes, you can," Bina said. She pried his massive hands open and deposited the gold pieces into his palms.

Tears came to his eyes, something Bina had only witnessed at Nathan's death. Reluctantly, he dropped the bands into a pouch hanging from his waist. Bina initiated their mutual hug. Flavius and Oren appeared. Palus pointed at them.

"You two take care of My Lady." Oren ran to him and gave him a hug. Palus returned the gesture and then with one swift motion, he leaped into the horse's saddle, pulled the reins, and headed away. He glanced back, waved and then sped on. Bina watched until he was out of sight, her arm draped around Oren's shoulders.

It was mid morning and the wagon was packed. Flavius was of great help and the king had made sure they had plenty of supplies for the trip back. A harness was rigged so that two horses could pull the wagon. Oren's horse was tied to the back of the wagon. Flavius rode along side of the wagon as Bina and Oren sat side by side. The long trek started.

They crossed the river near Ashdod and headed north near the shoreline to the Great Sea and reached the southern border of the tribe of Dan by the end of the first day. Ekron was on the border and they stayed at an inn there. Flavius, ever polite and discreet, insisted on staying in a separate room despite Bina telling him that was unnecessary.

By the end of the second day they were in the Plain of Sharon and camped in a grove of trees near the Great Sea. The third day they made only a short distance before a storm that blew in from the sea forced them to take refuge in a nearby small village to wait out the torrential rain.

The morning of the fourth day gave partly cloudy skies and they came to the point where Flavius would continue on north along the coast toward Dor while Bina and Oren would turn inland toward Taanach and finally through the pass at the Gilboa mountain range and thus to Shunem.

"Are you sure you don't want me to go to Shunem with you?" Flavius asked.

"I'm sure and it is out of your way. Besides we will be okay," Bina answered.

"It has been my pleasure to meet you. I wish you well and will always remember your great service to my king and all of Philistia."

"It is you we owe great thanks to for allowing us entrance to Gath. It put a roof over our heads and a chance to help you. I wish you safe passage and reuniting with your family," Bina said. Flavius thanked her and headed on north.

Bina and Oren reached Shunem in mid afternoon. As they approached their home, Oren made an observation.

"Mother, someone is living in our house."

"Yes, I am afraid so. It appears they have been tilling our fields and harvesting despite the famine."

Bina and Oren approached. A husky man and haggard woman met them.

"What business do you have here?" the man asked gruffly.

"This is our house and our land. The prophet, Elisha told us to leave and come back after the seven years of famine were over," Bina said.

"We found the house vacant four years ago and have tilled, planted, watered and harvested this land through the hardest of times. We are not leaving," the man said. With that he and his wife turned around and went back inside.

"Well, Oren, I didn't want to do this but we are going to have to take a trip to Jerusalem to get the king to give us our land back. The day is far spent but I think these Philistine horses can get us as far as Tirzah where we can spend the night."

Bina didn't like having to take this action but she could tell right off these people were not about to leave. She was a benevolent person but that attribute didn't apply in this case. Nathan, Palus and herself had lived here, worked hard, and helped the needy people of Shunem often, besides, Oren was born here too.

They arrived in Tirzah as the twilight overtook the fading day. The next day at mid afternoon their horses pulled their wagon almost effortlessly up the hill to Jerusalem. They spotted King Joram conversing with Elisha's servant, Gehazi. Bina gasped as she saw that

Gehazi was covered with leprosy, his skin being white as snow. She could hear the conversation. The king was asking Gehazi about Elisha's miraculous acts and mentioned her son being raised from the dead.

"O, King, there comes the woman from Shunem whose son Elisha raised from the dead," Gehazi said, pointing at Bina and Oren.

"I recognize you now. I gave you two horses over ten years ago," Joram said.

"Yes, O, King, and I am forever in your debt."

"Your fine reputation continues through my reign. How have you survived the seven years of famine?" Joram asked.

"The prophet, Elisha told me to leave until the seven years of famine were over. I chose to go to the land of the Philistines."

"Really? Did they accept you?"

"Yes, the king was very gracious."

"Your manner of dealing with people stretches far and wide," Joram said.

"It is a long story, but while we were gone, someone moved into our house and used our land for the past four years. They refuse to leave."

"You there, go with this great woman and make sure she gets her home and land back. She is to be restored all the fruits of her land back since the day she left." Joram pointed emphatically at a husky officer nearby. Quickly, Joram prepared a document, rolled it up, melted wax and sealed it with his ring.

"You are most gracious, O, King."

"It was my pleasure to see you again. I'm sure this will be the last time we meet this side of eternity. Everything is against me: being the son of Ahab, Jezebel as my mother, the Syrians ready to make war with us, Elisha's prophecies against me, the famine taking its toll of the people and worst yet, I believe Jehu may be the next king."

"My problems pale in comparison to yours, O, King," Bina said. Her sorrowful heart went out to him.

"I have been unable to overcome my terrible lineage. This will probably be my last act of decency," Joram said.

"I will pray for you," Bina said, knowing it was all she could offer.

"I pray you will prosper," Joram said.

"My Lady, may I go with you? I did a grievous wrong to Elisha and Naaman. This is why I am covered with leprosy. Because of my lying and greediness, Elisha transferred Naaman, the Syrian's leprosy, to me and my offspring forever," Gehazi said.

"I would welcome your company."

"Thank you. Of course I am no longer accepted by Elisha as his servant."

"Is there any possibility that Elisha would reverse his punishment of you if you showed you were reformed from the mistakes you made?"

They climbed aboard the wagon.

"Not likely," Gehazi answered.

"We can make Baalhazor by nightfall. Do you think Elisha would be at his home in Abelmeholah at this time?"

"I have no idea. Elisha does not confide in me anymore. Knowing your character I suspect you are going to try talking him into ridding me of this leprosy."

"In a manner of speaking."

"If you mean to take a detour to Abelmeholah, My Lady, that is alright. That is on our way to Shunem and the king will allow me to go with you," the king's officer said, as he rode alongside Bina's wagon.

"Thank you. I promise it will not take too long."

They stayed in Baalhazor and got an early start the next morning. They made Abelmeholah by noon. Gehazi knew the location of Elisha's home and they made their way through the narrow streets to his modest dwelling.

Elisha was just coming out the front door and seemed in a hurry. He spotted Bina and her wagon of passengers along with King Joram's officer.

"You have caught me just before I am to deliver some important prophecies. I have a long journey ahead of me," Elisha said.

"Please, Holy Prophet, this will take very little of your time. May I ask you a few questions?" Bina asked.

"Of course I will make time for you, My Lady," he said, and then glanced at Gehazi. Bina thought he could see sadness in his bearded expression and not anger.

"I have used one of the two healing gifts you gave me. It was for the Philistine king. I know that seems strange as they have been our enemies. He truly was kind and gracious to me."

"I have come to trust your judgment when it comes to character. That is why I imparted the gifts of healing two people," Elisha said.

"I hesitate to ask you and am afraid of your answer but. . ." She left it unsaid for a short duration.

"Out with it, My Lady. The Lord has not revealed to me what you leave unsaid. I remember not knowing your distress when your boy here had died. You are a complex woman but in a good way."

"As always, your words are most uplifting. I want to know if this last act of healing could properly be used to heal Gehazi of his leprosy." Bina held her breath but Gehazi cut in before Elisha could answer.

"My Lady! You must not ask such a question to my Master, Elisha. His pronunciation of punishment on me is permanent. I am not worthy to be cured."

"My Prophet, I must tell you that Gehazi told King Joram of your raising my son from the dead. That resulted in the king sending his officer with us to Shunem to recover my house, land and fruits of harvest as someone else has taken my property."

"It is a hard thing you ask, My Lady. Do you feel Gehazi has reformed?"

"Yes, I do. He has asked me if he could accompany me. While on our way here he requested if he could be my servant and help me with my land. I trust him to work alongside of Oren and me."

"I will trust your judgment once again. Your work in Philistia has already been proclaimed far and wide. That resulted in the saving of many lives." Elisha then turned to Gehazi and shook his staff at him.

"Gehazi, you can thank this great Shunammite woman and thank the Lord that she came into your life. If I hear you mistreat her, betray her, cheat her, or run away from her, I will know about it. This white leprosy you have will seem a blessing compared to what I will bring upon you. Have you heard of Job's affliction? It was what they called black leprosy. You don't want to experience that."

"Please no, My Lord. I have learned my lesson," Gehazi said and kneeled with his face almost touching the ground.

"My Lady, Bina, I have heard you called. Gehazi's heart I have always been able to read and I perceive your judgment accurate. You may use your final gift of healing on Gehazi. We will not record this in any manuscript. Now I must go and I wish all of you well," Elisha said and walked away.

"How can I ever thank you, My Lady?" Gehazi asked.

"By working hard on our land."

"I would ask you to wait until we get to Shunem before healing me?"

"Why?"

"It will be a special time for me to remember if you permit me to serve you the rest of my life in Shunem." Gehazi drew a deep breath and bowed his head.

"As you wish. Now let us hurry to Shunem."

When they arrived in Shunem, Joram's officer presented the sealed document from Joram to the people who had taken Bina's land. The man and his wife were scared out of their wits and wasted no time gathering their belongings, leaving the house cleaned and revealing all they had reaped during their four year stay. Bina thanked the officer and invited him to spend the night but he insisted he had to return to Jerusalem immediately. He mentioned concern that King Joram would probably be wounded in a battle with Syria and not survive Jehu's sword after that. He expressed he hoped he was wrong and Bina conveyed her hope for that too. It seemed the officer intended to ride through the night in order to reach Jerusalem as soon as possible.

Bina showed Gehazi the barn and her, Oren and Gehazi bedded down the horses and unloaded the wagon. It was Gehazi's insistence before he was healed. After they finished, they retired to the house.

"Are you ready to be healed, Gehazi?" Bina asked.

"Yes, My Lady." Oren stood by and watched intently.

"Stand before me then." Gehazi complied and breathed deeply, swallowing as Bina placed her hands on his shoulders. She also took a deep breath and felt in her body a comforting warmth as if her own physical being knew what was about to happen.

"Dear Lord, heal this poor soul of their disease, Amen."

She felt an out flowing, not a weakening of her but rather a strengthening just as it had with King Achish. She took that as a signal that she had made the right choice with her precious gift. As she stepped back, lifting her hands from Gehazi's shoulders, he was whole again. This was no slow bleeding away of the leprosy, but an instantaneous occurrence. Ghazi looked at his hands and touched his face. His expression gave way to a broad smile. He bowed and expressed himself.

"My Lady. Thank you from the depths of my soul." He dropped to his knees.

"Here now. There will be no worshipping of persons in this house. That should only be done to our Lord." She kneeled, took Gehazi's hands and gently urged him to stand.

The three of them labored together, Oren being thirteen now with the strength of a man, Gehazi tireless and faithful to Bina, and Bina herself working toward the possibility of once again helping those of Shunem.

END

JUST LIKE THAT SHUNAMMITE

BY

Fred McKinney

Numbers in parenthesis are verses in 2 Kings 4.

In You, O Lord, I put my trust; Your Word is my delight;

In you, O Lord, I long to be, just like that Shunammite.

Her noble deeds were virtuous, and tempered by her grace,

Her modesty and godliness adorned her dwelling place.

The Bible says that she was great; so great, long, long ago; (8)

Her character was well defined; her name, we do not know.

A prophet often passed her way, seen weary, worn, and beat;

The Shunammite would ask him in, to rest relax,
and eat.

And then, to help, she sought to build a "chamber"
down the hall; (10)

A room for him, when he passed by; built high upon the wall.

Her selfless acts of charity were far removed from
greed;

She simply sought to please the Lord, by helping
folks in need.

Gehazi said, "Please hear me, lord, the
Shunammite's alone;

She's barren, sir, and motherhood's a joy she's
never known." (14)

"Go fetch her now," Elisha said, *"for this thing
shall be done;"*

When she arrived, he said to her. "You shall
embrace a son." (16)

And it was so, a child was born; the prophecy came true; (17)

Prosperity and peace prevailed; but then, an ill-wind blew!

One dreadful day, the lad was sick; great pain throbbed in his head; (19)

His mother held him on her knees, till noon; and, he was **dead!** (20)

In just a while, the prophet said, *"Here comes that Shunammite;"* (25)

As she drew near, it seemed quite clear that something wasn't right?

Disquieted, and so distraught, she fell and grasped his feet; (27)

Then, he perceived her soul was vexed where death and sorrow meet!

"Did I ask you for a son?" 'No!' I said, *"Deceive me not!"* (28)

"O, prophet of the Lord Most High, was this to be

my lot?"

So, off they went down Carmel's slope,

……passing scenic rocks and rills; (30, 35)

And through the plains of Issachar, they drove on

toward the hills.

Gehazi, he'd been sent ahead, in his master's place;

(31)

And put Elisha's staff upon the little child's face;

He didn't bow; He didn't pray, he didn't do what's

right!

So, he returned, for he had failed to demonstrate

God's might.

And soon, they reached the woman's house; Elisha

led the way; (32)

He promptly sought the little child, a stone-cold

lump of clay.

The prophet closed his door and prayed for pow'r to raise the dead;

And mouth to mouth, and eye to eye, he stretched out on his bed. (34)

A miracle, by faith, transpired; **Praise God; the dead can rise!**

The little boy sneezed, seven times; then opened up his eyes. (35)

His soul came back; life was restored; it was an **awesome sight!**

And then, Elisha said, "Go, go;.....go get that Shunammite!"

Gehazi fetched her down the hall; and she came, on the run;

When she arrived, the prophet said, *"Come in; Pick up your son!"* (36)

But first, she bowed; with due respect, and then, she went on out. (37)

By faith, she'd put her trust in God, without despair and doubt.

This woman was a prototype, a yard-stick, that's a fact.

Her life is an example of how **all of us** should act.

For she was kind; so generous; she sought-out things to do;

She made the world a better place; and knew "contentment," too. (13)

Her noble deeds, she counted not; her hope soared up on High.

By faith, she knew that *"all was well,"* and so should You and I. (26)

Her name's unknown, her grave's obscure, yet, we can all recite:

"In you, O' Lord, I long to be: *JUST LIKE THAT SHUNAMMITE."*

Printed in Great Britain
by Amazon

34854997R00076